DINOFOURS™
IT'S VALENTINE'S DAY!

To Big Bo and Little Bo
— S.M.

Go to www.scholastic.com for Web site information on Scholastic authors and illustrators.

Text copyright © 2001 by Scholastic Inc.
Illustrations copyright © 2001 by Hans Wilhelm, Inc.
All rights reserved. Published by Scholastic Inc.
SCHOLASTIC, CARTWHEEL BOOKS, DINOFOURS, and associated logos
are trademarks and/or registered trademarks of Scholastic Inc.

Library of Congress Cataloging-in-Publication Data
Metzger, Steve.
    Dinofours, it's Valentine's Day! / by Steve Metzger ; illustrated by Hans Wilhelm.
        p. cm
    "Cartwheel books."
    Summary: The Dinofours keep their teacher busy helping them make Valentine's Day cards for their families and friends, until they realize that they want to show her how much they love her.
    ISBN 0-439-17960-2 (pbk.)
        [1. Valentines — Fiction. 2. Valentine's Day — Fiction. 3. Nursery schools — Fiction. 4. Schools — Fiction.
        5. Teachers — Fiction. 6. Dinosaurs — Fiction.] I. Wilhelm, Hans, 1945- ill. II. Title.
    PZ7.M56775 Dig 2001
    [E] — dc21   00-035813

12 11 10 9 8 7 6 5 4 3 2   01 02 03 04 05
                                                                                               24
                            Printed in the U.S.A.
                        First printing, January 2001

DINOFOURS™
IT'S VALENTINE'S DAY!

by Steve Metzger
Illustrated by Hans Wilhelm

Cartwheel BOOKS®

SCHOLASTIC INC.
New York   Toronto   London   Auckland   Sydney
Mexico City   New Delhi   Hong Kong

It was Valentine's Day!

The children were getting ready to make Valentine's Day cards for their mothers, fathers, grandparents, sisters, brothers, baby-sitters, and friends.

"Brendan, would you like to make a Valentine's Day card for someone?" Mrs. Dee asked.

"I'm too busy building a big house," Brendan replied. "I'll make one later."

Mrs. Dee turned to the other children.

"Does anyone need help?"
she asked.

"I do, Mrs. Dee," Danielle said.
"Please write the words
*Happy Valentine's Day, Mommy.
I love you* on my card."

"Okay, Danielle," Mrs. Dee said. Just as she began writing, she heard Tara say to Tracy, "You're too close! Your arm is touching my card."

"No, it's not," said Tracy.

"I'll be right back, Danielle," Mrs. Dee said.

As soon as she moved Tracy's chair away from Tara's, Mrs. Dee heard Joshua say, "Mrs. Dee! My scissors won't cut!"

Mrs. Dee took a new pair of scissors from the art shelf. As soon as she handed them to Joshua, she heard Danielle say, "Mrs. Dee! Mrs. Dee! You didn't finish writing my words!"

"I'm sorry," said Mrs. Dee, moving over to Danielle. "I was busy helping Joshua."

Mrs. Dee helped Danielle with her card. As soon as she finished, she heard, "I'm hungry!" It was Brendan.

"It's not Snack Time yet, but it will be soon," Mrs. Dee said. "Would you like to make your Valentine's Day card now?" she asked.

"I'll make it later," Brendan replied.

"Mrs. Dee! Mrs. Dee!" Tracy called out. "How do you spell *Mommy*?"

"Please try to sound it out," said Mrs. Dee.
"What letter do you think it starts with?"
"M!" Tracy said. "What's next?"
Before Mrs. Dee could continue, she heard Albert say,
"My card is too small. Everyone else has a bigger card."

"Are you sure, Albert?" Mrs. Dee asked. "I made plenty of big hearts."

"But mine is small," said Albert. "I need a big heart for my baby-sitter."

"Okay," said Mrs. Dee as she cut out a big construction-paper heart for Albert. As soon as she finished, she heard Danielle say, "Mrs. Dee, please write down the words for my card."

"I thought I already wrote your words," said Mrs. Dee.

"Those were the words for my *mommy's* card," Danielle said. "I want you to help me write my *daddy's* card."

"Okay, Danielle," Mrs. Dee sighed. "I'll be right there."

Before she reached Danielle, she heard Joshua say, "Tara, you spilled glitter on my card. You messed it up."

"I didn't mean to," said Tara. "It was an accident."

"No, it wasn't!" Joshua said.

Mrs. Dee walked over to Tara and Joshua. But before she could settle their problem, she heard Tracy's voice.

"Mrs. Dee, what comes after M?" asked Tracy. "I'm still waiting for the next letter."

"And I'm waiting for you to write the words for my daddy's card," Danielle added.

Mrs. Dee sat down.

"Everybody, please be patient," she said. "First I'll help Tara and Joshua, then Tracy, and then I'll work with Danielle. I'm only one person."

Mrs. Dee looked up at the clock.

"Soon, we'll have our clean-up," she announced. "And then it will be time for snacks. So, please finish making your Valentine's Day cards."

"Oh, no!" shouted Brendan as he jumped up. "I didn't make my card yet. I need to make one for my mommy."

Brendan dashed over to the art table and sat down.

"Mrs. Dee! Mrs. Dee!" Brendan shouted. "I need markers, scissors, glue, glitter, ribbon, pencils, crayons, and the biggest heart in the whole world!"

Albert watched as Mrs. Dee helped Tara, Joshua, Tracy, and Danielle. When she began to help Brendan, Albert called the other Dinofours to the Dramatic Play area.

"Mrs. Dee is helping us make Valentine's Day cards for everyone else," Albert told them. "But no one is making a card for her."

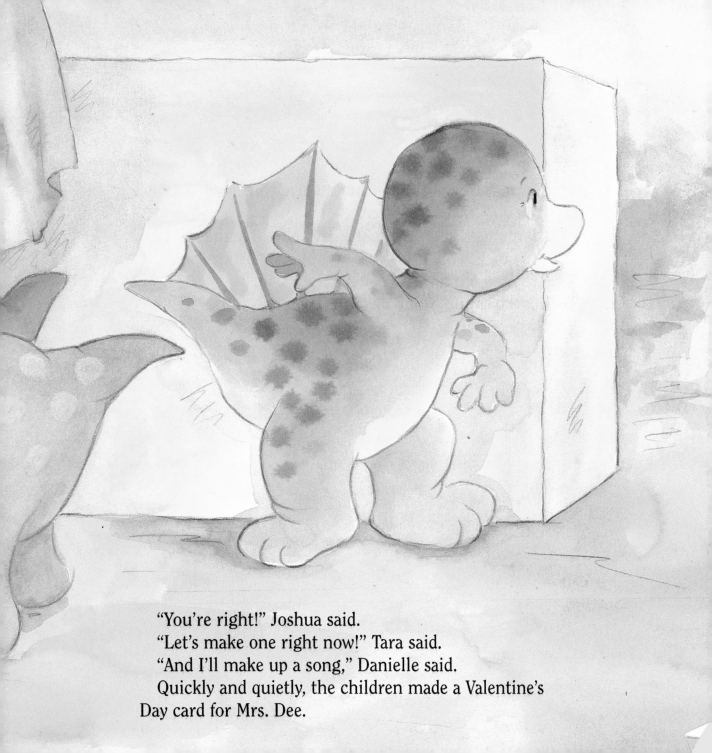

"You're right!" Joshua said.

"Let's make one right now!" Tara said.

"And I'll make up a song," Danielle said.

Quickly and quietly, the children made a Valentine's Day card for Mrs. Dee.

As soon as Mrs. Dee helped Brendan finish his card, she said, "Now it's time to clean up and get ready for Snack Time."

"No, Mrs. Dee," said Albert. "Not yet!"

"Why not?" she asked.

"Because we have something to give you," said Tracy.

"You do?" asked Mrs. Dee.

"Here it is!" said Tara as she gave Mrs. Dee the card.

"It's our Valentine's Day card for you," Joshua said.

"We used our favorite colors," Tara said.

"It's a beautiful rainbow," Mrs. Dee said. "I love it!"

"Now here's a song," Tracy said.
Together they all sang Danielle's song:

Mrs. Dee, Mrs. Dee,
Here's a card for you.
We want to tell you how we feel,
We love you, yes we do!

"Thank you all so much," Mrs. Dee said. "This means so
much to me."
Suddenly, Mrs. Dee noticed that someone was missing.
"Where's Brendan?" she asked.

"I'm over here!" Brendan said as he walked over from the
snack table. He handed Mrs. Dee a heart-shaped cracker.
"Happy Valentine's Day!"
    Everybody laughed...especially Mrs. Dee.